Magic Ballerina

Rosa and the Magic Moonstone

Welcome to the world of Enchantia!

I have always loved to dance. The captivating
music and wonderful stories of ballet are so
inspiring. So come with me and let's follow
Rosa on her magical adventures in
Enchantia, where the stories of dance will
take you on a very special journey.

p.s. Turn to the back to learn a special
dance step from me...

Special thanks to
Linda Chapman and
Nellie Ryan

First published in Great Britain by HarperCollins *Children's Books* 2009
HarperCollins *Children's Books* is a division of HarperCollins *Publishers* Ltd,
77-85 Fulham Palace Road, Hammersmith, London W6 8JB

The HarperCollins website address is
www.harpercollins.co.uk

1

Text copyright © HarperCollins *Children's Books* 2009
Illustrations copyright © HarperCollins *Children's Books* 2009

MAGIC BALLERINA™ and the 'Magic Ballerina' logo are
trademarks of HarperCollins Publishers Ltd.

ISBN 978 0 00 785917 7

Printed and bound in England by
Clays Ltd, St Ives plc

Mixed Sources
Product group from well-managed
forests and other controlled sources
www.fsc.org Cert no. SW-COC-1806
© 1996 Forest Stewardship Council

FSC is a non-profit international organisation established to promote the
responsible management of the world's forests. Products carrying the FSC
label are independently certified to assure consumers that they come
from forests that are managed to meet the social, economic and
ecological needs of present and future generations.

Find out more about HarperCollins and the environment at
www.harpercollins.co.uk/green

Magic Ballerina™

Rosa and the Magic Moonstone

Darcey Bussell

HarperCollins *Children's Books*

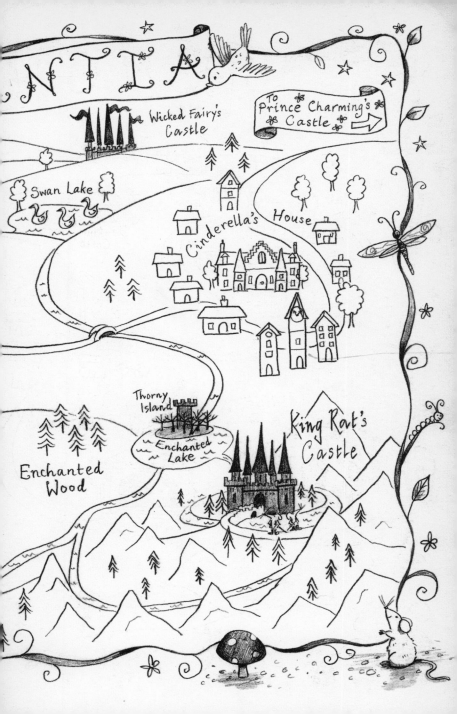

To Phoebe and Zoe, as they are the inspiration
behind Magic Ballerina.

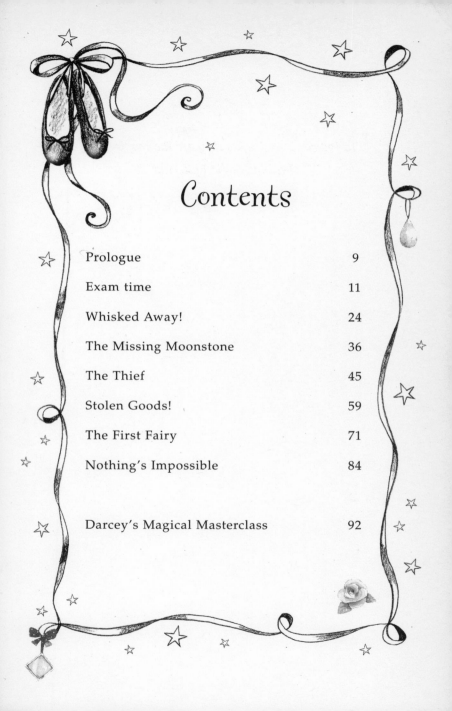

Contents

Prologue

In the soft, pale light, the girl stood
with her head bent and her hands
held lightly in front of her.
There was a moment's silence and then
the first notes of the music began.
For as long as the girl could remember
music had seemed to tell her of
another world – a magical, exciting
world – that lay far, far away.
She always felt if she could just
close her eyes and lose herself,
then she would get there.
Maybe this time. As the music
swirled inside her, she swept
her arms above her head, rose on to
her toes and began to dance...

Exam Time

The group of girls crowded into the changing rooms, chattering loudly.

"I can't believe we're going to be doing the exam *tomorrow*!" Olivia said.

"I know," replied Rebecca. "I'm really nervous."

"I'm scared stiff," agreed Asha.

Rosa Maitland looked at her friends in

surprise. "But why?" She twirled round before sitting down and starting to untie the ribbons on her red ballet shoes. "I'm looking forward to it."

Rosa loved dancing in front of people. She didn't care whether it was her teacher, Madame Za-Za, an audience at a theatre or an examiner in the ballet studio. She just loved to dance!

"But what if we go wrong?" said Olivia. "What if we forget everything?"

"Why would we?" Rosa said. "We're just doing the same exercises we do every lesson for Madame Za-Za. Stop worrying about it."

She got changed out of her leotard and after saying goodbye to Olivia and the others, she headed home. Rosa only lived around the corner. As she let herself into the house, her mum came into the hall in her wheelchair. Mrs Maitland had once been a ballerina, but then a car accident had ended her career. She still loved ballet, though, and often helped Rosa.

"How did the exam practice go?" she asked.

"Great." Rosa smiled as she remembered.

"It was cool dancing with a proper pianist playing and Madame Za-Za said I did my dances really well."

Mrs Maitland nodded. "How about your *barre* work?"

"Easy peasy!" grinned Rosa. She took hold of the kitchen door handle with her left hand and raised her leg to the *retiré* position,

bringing her right arm above her head, just like she would have to do in the exam. "Everyone else is really nervous, but I don't know why. I'm sure we're all going to pass."

Her mum looked anxious. "Rosa, it's really great you're not worried about the exam, but remember things can go wrong. If they do you must just keep on going and not give up. Don't expect to get everything right."

Rosa smiled confidently. "I'll be fine!" She danced into the kitchen. "What's for tea, Mum?"

"Pasta," said Mrs Maitland, following her. "Will you set the table, please, while I heat the sauce?"

Rosa nodded and started to get the

cutlery out. "What mark do you think I'll get for the exam?" she wondered.

Her mum smiled. "I don't know, sweetheart. But so long as you try your hardest, I'll be proud of you."

In bed that night, Rosa ran through the exercises she was going to have to do in her exam. Madame Za-Za had explained that the girls would go in groups of four. First they would do *barre* work, like they did every week in class, then they would go into the centre of the studio and do some more exercises there. After that they would take it in turns to do a set dance and then they had character work to do. Rosa had

practised over and over again. What mark would she get? The highest grade you could get was an A, which was also called distinction, and then it went B for merit, C for pass and if you didn't get any of those you failed. She really hoped she would do well.

She reached out to turn her bedside light off. As she did so, her eyes fell on the red ballet shoes hanging at the end of her bed. She smiled. They were her most precious things in the whole world. They were made of soft red leather and fitted her feet perfectly, but that wasn't why they were so special. They were special because they

17

were magic! Sometimes they would start
to sparkle and glow and then they would
whisk her off to Enchantia, a magic land
where all the characters from the
different ballets lived. Rosa had been on
some brilliant adventures there already.
She had met the King and Queen, made
friends with a fairy called Nutmeg and
her older sister, Sugar, the Sugar Plum Fairy.
She had come up against some pretty
horrible characters too – like King Rat
and the Wicked Fairy. But most of the
people who lived in Enchantia were really
nice.

Rosa snuggled down under her duvet.
She bet no one in Enchantia had to do
exams. When would she go there again?

She hugged her arms around herself. She
hoped it would be soon!

In the morning, Rosa arrived at the ballet
school early. She got changed into her
leotard and smoothed her wavy blonde hair
back into a neat bun. She was beginning to
feel slightly nervous. She was ready before
the other girls arrived, warming up by
doing *pliés*, holding lightly
on to one of the sinks as if
it was the *barre*.

"Hi," Olivia called
over. Her face was pale
and her eyes looked
wide and frightened.

Rosa saw her fingers shaking as she started to pull down the zip on her coat.

"It'll be OK," Rosa told her. She stretched her left foot out in front of her and lifted it quickly upwards as she practised a *grande battement*.

Back still, knees tight… the things to remember ran through her head as she lowered her foot slowly to the floor.

"I feel like I'm going to be sick," said Olivia.

"Me too," said Rebecca, sitting down beside her.

"And me," said Asha, looking alarmed. "What happens if we *are* sick in the exam?"

As she spoke the door opened and Madame Za-Za came in. As usual, the ballet

teacher was wearing a long ballet skirt, bangles and necklaces. Her greying hair

was tied back in a bun. She caught Asha's words. "You will not be sick, Asha," she said in her slight Russian accent. She smiled. "You will go into the exam room and perform your very best. I am sure all of you are going to make me proud. Now, when you're ready, please come to studio two and start to warm up."

Rosa hurried eagerly through the door.

Half an hour later, Rosa stood with Olivia, Asha and Rebecca in the corridor, waiting for Madame Za-Za to tell them they could go into the studio where the examiner was. They were going to be the first group in. Rosa was glad. She wanted to get started. Each of the four girls had a different

coloured ribbon pinned to her chest so the examiner would know who was who. Each of them was also holding the skirts and shoes they would need for their character work at the end.

"Does my hair look OK?" Rosa asked Olivia.

Olivia nodded. "How about mine?"

"You look great!" Rosa squeezed her hand. "Good luck!"

"You too!" Olivia said nervously.

Madame Za-Za held the door open. A bell rang inside the room. "In you go, girls."

Taking a deep breath, Rosa followed Asha, Rebecca and Olivia into the studio. The exam was about to begin!

Whisked Away!

Rosa and the other girls put down their shoes and skirts at the side of the room and curtsied to the examiner who was beside a small table. The examiner, a small slim woman, smiled and looked at their ribbons. "Good morning, girls. Let me just check I have your names and colours right. Asha – pink, Rebecca – blue,

Olivia – yellow and Rosa – white?"

They all nodded.

"Excellent. Take your places at the *barre*, please."

As they began to go through their exercises, Rosa felt happy and relaxed. She remembered to keep her back straight, her chin up, her hips still and her movements smooth. She wished she could look over at the others and see how they were doing, but she was concentrating too hard. She enjoyed stretching every muscle as much as she could, keeping her arm movements flowing and graceful.

After working at the *barre* they went to the centre of the studio. The first few exercises went well. *I'm really doing OK,*

Rosa thought, as they got ready to start their pirouette exercises. *I wonder what mark I'll get. Mum would be so pleased if I...*

Suddenly she realised that she had been distracted and the examiner had told them all to start. The others were already turning. She quickly tried to join in, but wobbled badly as she came to a stop. She glanced at the examiner, hoping she hadn't noticed, but the examiner was looking directly at her. Rosa blushed. Oh no. She'd really messed that exercise up!

The next exercise was *changements* – jumps where their feet swapped position in the air. Usually Rosa could do them easily but, feeling flustered still, she lost her balance. It went from bad to worse. In

every exercise she seemed
to make a mistake and
the harder she tried,
the worse it got. Her
arms and legs felt
wrong, her jumps
felt rushed and her
landings were
unbalanced. By the
time they finished
working in the centre,
Rosa's cheeks were blazing.
She didn't think she had ever done her
exercises so badly.

Her eyes prickled with tears as she lined
up with the others at one end of the studio
for the set dance. *I'm going to fail for sure,*

she thought, brushing away her tears. The music started and Asha began. She danced lightly across the floor, her elegance making Rosa feel worse than ever.

I'm not going to get a distinction or a merit. I'm not even going to pass. Mum's going to be

so upset with me and what's Madame Za-Za going to say? Maybe she'll make me go down to a different class!

It was impossible. She'd never pass. She didn't want to do the set dance and the character work now. Wild ideas filled her head. Maybe she should just say she was sick and leave. She just wanted to run out of the room.

Asha finished the dance and Rebecca began.

Suddenly Rosa's feet started to tingle. She glanced down at her shoes. They were glowing! She caught her breath. She must be about to go to Enchantia! Luckily she knew that not even a second would pass in the real world while she was away in the

29

magic land, so no one in the room would notice she had gone.

A rainbow of bright colours started to swirl around her and the next minute she felt herself lifted into the air and whisked away.

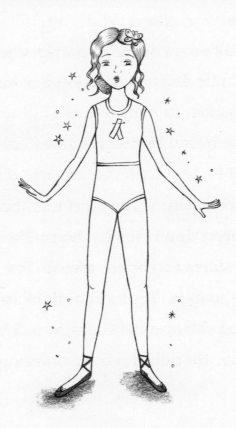

Rosa spun round and round until the magic gently lowered her down. She blinked as the swirl of colours faded. She was sitting in an empty theatre. It was dark and the heavy curtains were drawn across the stage.

She rubbed a couple of half-dry tears from her cheeks, trying to get her head round the fact that she wasn't in the exam room any more. Where was she? She knew she must be in Enchantia, but she'd landed in the wood before, never in this theatre.

Just then the air filled with music and the curtains started to open, revealing a brightly-lit stage. A girl in a nightdress danced on. Maybe it's Clara from *The Nutcracker*, thought Rosa, wondering what was happening. But then she saw that the girl wasn't holding a nutcracker doll, she was holding a pumpkin! She was followed by a group of soldiers who looked like they were also from *The Nutcracker*. They were fighting a group of dancing giant sweets. *But in the ballet they fight an army of mice*, thought Rosa.

Before she had time to say anything, the soldiers had danced off the stage and a girl in rags had come on. *Cinderella!* thought Rosa. A beautiful fairy spun on after her. But it wasn't Cinderella's Fairy Godmother, it was Sugar, the Sugar Plum Fairy! Two more people followed them. They were dancing a *pas de deux*. One of them was a

beautiful girl with long dark hair who looked like Sleeping Beauty. Rosa stared. Sleeping Beauty wasn't dancing with her handsome prince, though, instead she was dancing with a surprised-looking Puss in Boots!

What's going on? Rosa wondered. *All the ballets seem to be completely mixed up!*

The curtain started to close. Rosa jumped to her feet. "Wait!" she called. She hurried out of the row of seats. But the curtains had shut.

Rosa hesitated, trying to decide what she should do when suddenly there was a tinkling of music and a fairy with dark hair wearing a pale brown and pink tutu danced on to the stage, travelling and turning with every step.

"Nutmeg!" cried Rosa, recognising her friend. She ran down the aisle to the stage. "Nutmeg! It's you!"

"Oh, Rosa!" the fairy stopped in perfect balance, her arms out to the sides. "I'm so glad you're here! We're in trouble again."

Rosa knew the red shoes only brought her to Enchantia when there was a problem to be solved. "Why?"

Nutmeg took a deep breath. "It's a long story. Come and sit down and I'll explain…"

The Missing Moonstone

Rosa and Nutmeg sat down on the edge of the stage. "So, what's happening, Nutmeg?" asked Rosa.

"King Tristan's magical moonstone ring has been stolen," replied Nutmeg. "It's a very special ring. It was given to him by the First Fairy of Enchantia, the fairy who was here when all the ballets were created. The

moonstone keeps all the stories in order and makes them work as they should. Since it's been missing none of the ballets have been right."

"I saw everything going wrong," said Rosa. "I couldn't work out what was happening."

"It's awful," said Nutmeg. "Everything's all mixed up."

"Why don't you just get the ring back?" asked Rosa. "Then everything would be all right again."

"It's not that simple," Nutmeg sighed. "We don't know who stole it, you see. Someone pretending to be a magical jeweller tricked the ring from the King. He said he had been sent by the First Fairy to clean it. As soon as he had the ring in his hands he vanished. Look. I can show you."

Nutmeg stood up and touched her wand to the ground. A pale pink mist appeared.

Rosa gasped as she saw a picture start to form inside it! It showed King Tristan in the courtyard of the Royal Palace. He was talking to a figure wrapped in a black cloak. As Rosa watched, the King took a gold ring with a sparkling white stone off his finger. He handed it to the cloaked figure. Then the figure spun round and vanished in a bright flash of light.

Rosa frowned when she caught sight of something poking out from underneath the black cloak – a long thin tail. It was only there for a second before it vanished.

"Did you see that?" she cried as Nutmeg touched the mist and it cleared.

"What?" asked Nutmeg.

"There was a tail sticking out from under the cloak!"

"Let me see." Nutmeg tapped the floor again and the mist reappeared. Within seconds she and Rosa were watching the vision repeating itself. This time Nutmeg gasped too. "You're right!"

They looked at each other.

"There's only one person that can be," said Rosa. "It must be King Rat! He must have taken the ring!"

"But why?" said Nutmeg.

"There's only one way to find out," replied Rosa bravely. "Let's go to his castle and see."

"But the mouse guards are so scary, and what if King Rat finds us," Nutmeg protested. "You know how much he hates people who dance and he doesn't like us at all after we stopped his last wicked plan."

"It doesn't matter. We have to get the ring back." Rosa took her friend's hand and looked into her brown eyes. "We can do this, Nutmeg. We've  stopped King Rat before and we can do it again. I know we can!"

Nutmeg took a deep breath. "OK, then, let's go!"

Nutmeg used her magic to take her and Rosa to the woods outside King Rat's castle. King Rat's magic was very powerful and he had placed enchantments on his castle grounds so that no one else could use strong magic there.

Rosa peered through the trees at the foreboding castle. King Rat had an army of human-sized mice who worked for him. They had pointed teeth and sharp swords.

"I can't see anyone—" She broke off as suddenly, the castle doors opened and the mouse guards came out. But they didn't look frightening at all. They came skipping out like school children – some were throwing balls at each other, others started to play hopscotch, three of them sat down to play a game of marbles, while another group played with some shiny trains and one played with a baby doll.

Rosa and Nutmeg exchanged astonished looks.

"What's going on?" whispered Nutmeg.

"They must have been caught up in the magical mix-up too," said Rosa.

"Of course! They're acting as if they're the children in *The Nutcracker*!" said Nutmeg.

Suddenly there was a loud burst of music. The door flew open and two figures came dancing out of the castle. One was the Nutcracker Soldier, dressed in his red and gold finery and the other…

Rosa stared at the person being twirled round and round, his expression outraged.

It was King Rat!

The Thief

The Nutcracker Soldier swung round in a joyful dance. King Rat's crown was now slipping to the side of his head and his cloak was hanging off one shoulder. "Get off me! GET OFF!" he was shouting, trying to pull himself free. But the Nutcracker simply twirled him faster across the grass.

Rosa started to giggle. "It looks like King

Rat's been caught in the mix-up too!"

The Nutcracker let go of King Rat and leaped dramatically into the air with a *grand jeté* before dancing away.

King Rat shook his fist at him. Then he straightened his crown and looked round at his usually fierce mice. Seeing them all

playing games, he buried his head in his paws.

"It doesn't look like he's having much fun," Rosa whispered quickly to Nutmeg. "Maybe he'll decide he wants to give the ring back."

"But how do we find out?" the fairy asked.

Rosa hesitated and then made a brave decision. She walked out of the trees!

She heard Nutmeg gasp. "What are you doing?"

Rosa ignored her.

King Rat saw Rosa and pointed in astonishment. "It's you! The dratted girl with the ballet shoes! And you've got that annoying fairy with you," he said as

Nutmeg ran to join Rosa. "How dare you both come to my castle uninvited!"

"I hope you've got a plan, Rosa!" Nutmeg whispered in a quavering voice as King Rat strode towards them. His fur was a greasy black and he had a long pointed nose and red eyes.

"Guards, get them!" he yelled. But the guards were too busy playing with their toys.

Rosa's heart pounded in her chest as she stared bravely at the rodent. "We know you've got the King's ring and we want it back." She thought about the look of horror on King Rat's face as the Nutcracker had danced with him. "You don't want the ballets mixed up any more than anyone else does. Give us the ring and then when it's returned to the King, everything will be all right again."

King Rat glared back at her. "Idiot girl! If it was that simple, don't you think I'd have given it back already?" He shook his head. "I can't give it back. It's broken."

"Broken!" Nutmeg exclaimed in horror.

King Rat's shoulders slumped. "That's why everything has gone wrong. If I still had it and it was all in one piece everything would be fine. But it's smashed to smithereens."

"How?" demanded Rosa.

"I dropped it," admitted King Rat. "It broke and then from that moment on, everything started going wrong." He reached into the pocket of his cloak and took out a small bag before shaking out a gold ring. It had a sparkling white stone that had obviously been glued together. There was one piece missing. "I couldn't find the last fragment."

"This is awful!" said Nutmeg. "If the

stone is broken, everything's going to stay mixed up forever!"

"I know," agreed King Rat gloomily. "I wish I'd never taken it. I only wanted it because it was so bright and shiny. Now life in Enchantia is never going to be the same again."

"There's nothing we can do," said Nutmeg, starting to cry.

Rosa put her arm around her friend and gave her a hug. "We can't give up that easily. Maybe *we* can find the missing piece of the ring." She looked at King Rat. "Where did you drop it?"

"Over there," he said, pointing back to the steps by the front door.

"Well, let's get looking!" said Rosa.

Rosa, Nutmeg and King Rat hunted around. The mouse guards nearby were arguing. "You must have taken my train! It was here a minute ago," said one. "You just wanted it because it was so shiny!"

"I didn't take it! I didn't!" said the second mouse.

"Did too!" whinged the first.

"Did not!"

Rosa began to think she preferred the guards when they were scary!

"Oh, this is useless! We've looked everywhere," King Rat said grumpily after ten minutes. He sat down in the shade of a nearby tree with massive leaves and took off his shoes with a groan. "My feet are killing me from all the dancing that the Nutcracker keeps making me do. I'm going to have a rest." He leaned against the tree trunk and closed his eyes.

"Maybe we should just give up,"
Nutmeg said to Rosa.

"No! The missing bit of stone can't have
just disappeared," said Rosa as King Rat
started to snore loudly. "Let's keep looking."

Nutmeg laid her wand down on the
ground and crouched on her hands and knees,
examining every inch of the grass. Rosa
joined in too, but no matter how much they
hunted, they couldn't find the missing piece.

Nutmeg sighed. "It's no use, Rosa," she said, getting to her feet at last. "We're not going to find it. We—" she broke off. "Where's my wand? I left it here!" She pointed at the ground. "It's gone!"

"It can't have gone," said Rosa.

Nutmeg turned on King Rat, who was just waking up. "Have you taken my wand?" she demanded.

"What would I want with your stupid sparkly wand!" snorted King Rat. He got to his feet and reached for his boots. He gave a yell. "Hey! Someone's stolen the buckle off my boot!" He swung round to Nutmeg. "Give it back!"

"It wasn't me. I haven't touched your smelly boot!" said Nutmeg. "You're just

saying that because you took my wand."

"I didn't take it!"

"You must have!"

"Stop it, both of you!" Rosa broke in.
"Nutmeg hasn't taken the buckle off your
boot," she said to King Rat. "She's been
with me, looking for the missing piece of
the moonstone all the time you've been

asleep. And King Rat can't have taken your wand," she said to the fairy. "He's been snoring away like anything."

"I do not snore!" said King Rat indignantly.

Rosa ignored him. "There has to be another explanation."

Just then there was a shout from the guards and a flash of black and white as a bird swooped across the courtyard and flew up into the tree with the big green leaves.

"My marble! My best shiny marble! That bird took it!" shouted one of the mice.

Of course! *A magpie!*

Rosa grinned at Nutmeg and King Rat.
"You know, I think we might just have
found the thief!"

Stolen Goods!

"Magpies often steal shiny things," Rosa explained to King Rat and Nutmeg. She looked up into the branches of the tree with the big leaves. "I bet he's got a nest in that tree. If we could get up to it, we'd probably find your wand and the buckle and all kinds of other things."

Nutmeg turned to King Rat. "If you lift

that spell of yours that stops me using
magic, I could fly up there and see," she
said, fluttering her wings.

King Rat hesitated.

"You want your buckle back, don't you?"
Rosa said to him.

"Oh, all right. What harm can it do?"
King Rat held up his paws and muttered a
spell under his breath.

Nutmeg spun round and rose into the air.
She flew up into the tree. The magpie
squawked from one of the branches.

"There is a nest up here but these leaves
are so big I can hardly see it!" Nutmeg
called down to Rosa and King Rat. She had
to pull a few of the leaves off to get to the
nest. They floated down to the ground.

"Can you see anything yet?" called Rosa.

"Yes! Here's my wand, and King Rat's buckle, marbles and a train and—" Nutmeg broke off with a gasp. "Oh, goodness! Wait until you see this!"

She flew down and landed lightly on her pointes, her arms full of the things she had found. She quickly handed back the buckle, the train and the marble, slipped her wand into a pocket in her tutu and then held out her hand. "Look!" Slowly, she opened her fingers.

Rosa held her breath. *Could it be... was it really...?* "It's the missing piece of moonstone!" she gasped.

Nutmeg beamed. "The magpie must have taken it as well!"

"Where's the ring?" Rosa quickly asked King Rat.

"Here." He held it out.

Rosa took it and quickly added the

missing piece. It fitted
perfectly! The ring
was complete
again.

She glanced round, expecting something
to happen – some music or some magic. But
everything stayed exactly the same. The
guards kept playing as if they were
children.

"Maybe we need some glue!" King Rat
hurried inside and came back with a tube.
He carefully stuck the piece of stone into
the ring, but *still* nothing happened.

"Why's it not working?" said Rosa.

Nutmeg bit her lip. "I think I might
know. I remember when I was little, people
said that if the ring was ever broken it

could only be mended by the First Fairy
coming back to Enchantia. I thought it was
just a story, but maybe it is real."

"Well, how can we get her to come here?"
Rosa asked.

"The only way to do it is to get at least
one person from every ballet to join in a
dance," Nutmeg answered.

"We can't do that," said King Rat. "There
are too many ballets."

Even Rosa felt stumped. How could they
possibly get one person from every ballet
together? "Oh," she said, her heart sinking.
"That's going to be impossible, isn't it?
We'd have to travel round for days and
days."

"Hang on!" Nutmeg said, suddenly

seizing her hands, her eyes shining. "It's not impossible at all! In Enchantia we can summon anyone by doing a bit of their dance from the ballet they come from."

Rosa stared. "Really?"

"Yes! So I could dance and summon some people and then they could dance too and help us summon more people." Nutmeg twirled round in excitement.

"Soon we'd have everyone we need!"

"But… but that means there would be lots of people dancing!" King Rat exclaimed. "Here! Outside my castle!"

Nutmeg nodded.

"NO!" yelled King Rat, burying his head in his hands. "I'll never live this down!"

Ignoring King Rat, Rosa and Nutmeg hurried away. "I'll do the dancing to summon the first few people and as they arrive, you can explain what's happening and get them to dance too," said Nutmeg.

She waved her wand. Music flowed through the air. Rosa recognised it immediately. It was the Sugar Plum Fairy's

music from *The Nutcracker*. Nutmeg began
to dance. Rosa couldn't help herself, she
had to join in. She couldn't go up on her
pointes like Nutmeg but she moved
lightly across the grass, copying as best
she could. Nutmeg caught her eyes and
grinned at her.

A minute later there was a lilac flash, and Nutmeg's sister, the beautiful Sugar Plum Fairy, appeared. She was wearing a lilac tutu and had a sparkling tiara in her hair.

"Oh, not her too!" King Rat groaned from the castle.

"What's going on?" Sugar asked.

"Rosa will explain!" called Nutmeg, waving her wand again. The music changed to a sweet melody, full of longing. Nutmeg began to dance round, as if she was holding a broom in her hands.

"Cinderella's music!" cried Rosa. She turned to Sugar. "We're trying to summon a character from every single ballet," she explained. "So that we can do a dance to make the First Fairy appear!" Quickly she

told Sugar everything that had happened.

"I'll help!" Sugar said eagerly. She waved her own wand and began to do a dance that Rosa recognised as part of the swans' dance from *Swan Lake*. After a few minutes, three great white swans came flapping across the sky.

By now Cinderella had appeared and she had started to do the Lilac Fairy's dance from *Sleeping Beauty* and Nutmeg was dancing a new dance that Rosa had never seen before. Suddenly a rosy-cheeked girl in a bright costume appeared.

"Swanhilda from the ballet *Coppelia*," Sugar cried to Rosa as she twirled past, jumping into the air and summoning the Prince from *The Firebird*. "It's working, Rosa! It's really working! Everyone's coming!"

The First Fairy

Rosa's head spun with all the different music. Within minutes the area outside the castle had filled with people. They were all shouting out, asking what was going on. Rosa couldn't get round them all fast enough to explain.

"We've done it!" Sugar exclaimed. "We've got someone from every ballet!"

"Although half of them don't know why they're here yet," said Nutmeg, looking worried. "How are we going to tell them they all have to do a dance? They're being so noisy!"

"What we need is a megaphone, or something that would work as one!" said Rosa. What could they do? Her eyes fell on the enormous leaves that had fallen from the tree and an idea came to her. Hurrying over to one, she rolled it up into a cone-like shape.

She ran up the steps and shouted through it. "Quiet, please! QUIET!"

Gradually the noise died down. Rosa blushed as everyone turned to look at her. "I know some of you are wondering why

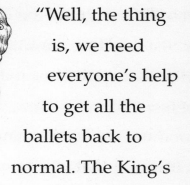

you're here," she said. "Well, the thing is, we need everyone's help to get all the ballets back to normal. The King's moonstone ring is broken and to mend it we need to summon the First Fairy." A buzz of excited chatter rose. She raised her voice again. "We need you all to do a dance and..." She broke off as she realised she didn't know what the dance was!

Sugar saw Rosa's confusion and jumped up beside her, taking the megaphone. "I can show you what to do, everyone. It's very simple. The important thing is that you all do it at the same time in a circle, and we keep doing it until the First Fairy appears."

She used her wand to make a lively tune play and then she ran down the steps and began to dance – three steps to the right, followed by a turn, another three steps, followed by another turn. "Copy me!" she called. "This is all you have to do!"

Everyone began to join in.

"Come on!" Nutmeg said, pulling Rosa into the dance.

Rosa's heart soared. She hadn't been sure if she would be included, not being a character from a ballet, but there was nothing she wanted more than to dance to the music. Dancing joyfully with the others in the circle, she lost herself in the

music, stepping
and turning,
stepping and
turning until her head
whirled.

*I wish the examiners
could see me now*, she
thought.

A new piece of
music broke in on
top of the first. It was different, slow and
gentle, piercingly sweet. It swelled in
loudness, gradually getting stronger. It gave
Rosa the feeling of dawn breaking in the
morning. The lively music faded
underneath it and gradually everyone
slowed down and stopped.

"Look!" Rosa breathed. In the centre of the circle a golden haze was forming. A figure appeared in the middle of it and the mist cleared. A beautiful fairy, dressed all in gold with a tiara on her pale blonde hair, was standing in a perfect *arabesque*, balanced on one toe, her other leg held straight out behind her, her arms stretched out. She looked like a bird caught in mid-flight.

Rosa felt like she never wanted to take her eyes off her. The fairy's face was beautiful, calm and serene, and the air around her seemed to sparkle. Everyone watched in awe as she slowly brought her leg down until her feet were together and then she turned on her pointes and looked straight at Rosa.

Dancing quickly with a fast-turning step, the First Fairy spun out of the centre of the circle and stopped in front of Rosa. She held out her wand and looked invitingly at her. Rosa didn't need her to say anything. She knew what she had to do. She held the ring out in front of her.

The fairy gracefully touched the moonstone with her wand. There was a

flash of golden light.
Rosa looked at it and
gasped. "It's mended!"

The music rose and swelled. The First
Fairy smiled and then she spun away
round the circle, dancing faster and faster.
As the music reached the final note, she
jumped into the air in a *grand jeté* and
vanished, leaving just a faint gold mist
shimmering behind her.

There was a moment's silence and then
suddenly everyone started to talk at once.

"It was the First Fairy!"

"She was really here!"

"And she mended the ring!"

"Are the ballets all right now?"

Rosa looked around. King Rat's guards

were slowly standing up. They looked dazed and confused.

"Marbles!" said one.

"Hopscotch!" said another, looking at the marks on the floor.

"Playing with dolls!" said a third, hastily throwing down the baby doll he had been cuddling. He made a big effort to snarl and look vicious. "What's going on? I *hate* dolls unless I'm chewing on them to sharpen my teeth! Yuck!"

"You're back to normal!" King Rat shouted in delight. "Yahoo!"

"Everything's back to normal!" said Sugar in relief.

The crowd of people cheered.

"Oh, Rosa. Thank you for helping us!" said Nutmeg, hugging her friend.

Sugar smiled at her. "We'd never have solved the problem without you, Rosa."

"I was sure it was impossible," said Nutmeg.

Rosa grinned. "Nothing's impossible," she said.

"Well, apart from maybe making King Rat like dancing!" Nutmeg giggled.

"Hmm." A mischievous twinkle lit up Sugar's eyes and for a moment the two sisters looked very similar. Sugar glanced to where King Rat was marching around yelling at his guards. "King Rat hasn't put his enchantment back yet that stops anyone doing magic here, has he?"

Nutmeg shook her head.

"Then let me see what I can do!" Sugar waved her wand.

A lively polka swelled through the air.

"Oh, not MORE dancing!" King Rat said, looking around as people cheered again and started to grab partners. They began to take light galloping sideways steps, swinging each other round.

Sugar danced over, pointed her wand at King Rat's boots and quickly said a magic spell:

"Boots twirl and spin, turn and prance,

   Make King Rat love to dance!"

"What? No!" King Rat yelled in horror as there was a lilac flash and suddenly his feet started to move of their own accord. But as he

began to spin
round, the horror
turned to surprise
and his mouth
turned upwards
in a grin.

"Actually,
this is quite
fun!" he
shouted. "I'm
dancing! Really dancing! Hey, wait
for me!" He galloped away with great
galumphing steps after the others, turning
round and round, his cloak flying out
behind him, his red eyes lit up with delight.

Rosa gasped. "So King Rat likes dancing
now!"

"Not forever, unfortunately. My magic's not strong enough for that. The spell will wear off after a bit." Sugar giggled. "But it will be fun watching him until it does!"

"Come on!" said Nutmeg, taking Rosa's hands. "Let's join in!"

They set off with Sugar dancing beside them. Rosa laughed in delight as they all swept around the castle in a laughing, happy throng. This was the best adventure ever! But then her feet started to tingle. Her ballet shoes were glowing.

"I'm about to go home!" she cried.

And in a whirl of sparkling colours, she felt herself being whisked away!

Nothing's Impossible

Rosa felt her feet hit the floor and the colours faded. She blinked. She was back in the exam room and Rebecca was dancing the set dance.

For a moment, Rosa felt dazed. So much had been happening in Enchantia that she had completely forgotten all about the exam. But now it came flooding back. *I've messed up*, she realised as Olivia started her dance. *I'm never going to pass.*

She felt a wave of despair. She wanted to give up. *No*, she thought, remembering what had just happened in Enchantia. *Nothing's impossible.*

Rosa took a deep breath. Maybe it was too late and she had failed already, but she had to try. She still had her set dance and character work to do. Maybe if she gave it her very best shot she still had a chance to pass.

Olivia finished and suddenly it was Rosa's turn. She danced forward. Usually when she danced she talked herself through the steps in her head, but she knew the steps so well from all her practising that her body seemed to take over, and this time she just danced. She spun and jumped and ended perfectly, one arm high, the other by her side, her shoulders down, her chin lifted, her body poised and graceful.

As the music stopped she relaxed, a huge grin spreading over her face. She'd done it! Whether she passed or not she knew she had tried her very best and that was all that really mattered.

Quickly she joined the others. Now there was just the character dance to go!

"Oh, wow!" Olivia gasped as the door shut behind them after the exam had finished. "You were amazing, Rosa! I've never seen you dance so well. Your set dance and character dance were brilliant!"

"Thanks," Rosa said in relief. "I really messed up in the centre, though."

"Well, I got so much wrong at the *barre*," said Asha.

"And I forgot the steps in the character dance," groaned Rebecca.

"I certainly won't have passed. It's impossible," said Rosa.

"Nothing's impossible. You should know that by now, Rosa," Madame Za-Za said

briskly, opening the door of the changing rooms. "Come along, girls." She ushered them into the changing rooms. "Don't worry about what you got wrong; everyone makes mistakes in an exam. No one is ever perfect. I'm sure you all did your best and that is the most important thing."

Two weeks later, Rosa arrived at the ballet school with Olivia. They were greeted at the door by Asha. "The exam results are up!" she exclaimed. "Quick! Come and see!"

Rosa and Olivia both hurried down the corridor. A piece of white paper was pinned to the noticeboard outside Madame Za-Za's office.

Rosa's heart pounded. She had been trying not to think about the exam. She knew she must have failed after making so many mistakes early on. She reached the notice, but the words seemed to swirl in front of her eyes as she tried to find her name.

Please let me have passed, please let me have passed, she prayed.

Olivia gave a massive squeal. "We both passed!" she said. "We did it! Look!" She pointed her finger at the paper and Rosa saw the words:

Olivia Rowley... A (distinction)

Rosa Maitland... A (distinction)

She had passed! And with distinction! She could hardly believe it.

She hugged Olivia. "Oh, wow! Oh, wow! Oh, wow!"

Madame Za-Za came out of her office and smiled at them. "Well done, girls. I'm very proud of you both."

"Thank you, Madame Za-Za!" Olivia gasped.

Madame Za-Za's eyes met Rosa's. "You see. As long as you never give up, nothing is impossible, Rosa," she said softly.

And in that moment, Rosa knew that she was right.

Darcey's Magical Masterclass

The Spell of the First Fairy

The First Fairy saved Enchantia with her spell to fix the moonstone. In the steps below try imaging that you are holding her wand as you move your arm around in graceful sweeping movements.

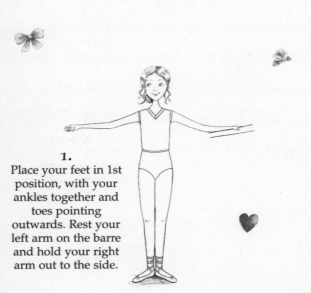

1.
Place your feet in 1st position, with your ankles together and toes pointing outwards. Rest your left arm on the barre and hold your right arm out to the side.

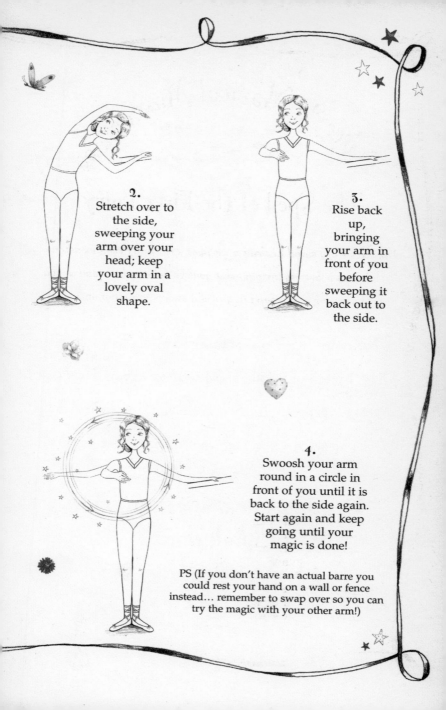

2.
Stretch over to the side, sweeping your arm over your head; keep your arm in a lovely oval shape.

3.
Rise back up, bringing your arm in front of you before sweeping it back out to the side.

4.
Swoosh your arm round in a circle in front of you until it is back to the side again. Start again and keep going until your magic is done!

PS (If you don't have an actual barre you could rest your hand on a wall or fence instead… remember to swap over so you can try the magic with your other arm!)

The ruler of the underwater kingdom has accused King Tristan of taking his special sceptre and has cast a storm spell over Enchantia until it's returned! Will Rosa be able to find out who really has the sceptre?

Read on for a sneak preview of book ten...

The silvery light cleared and Rosa saw that she was by the sea. The waves were stormy and grey and a cold wind was whipping through her hair. Rosa shivered and looked around. She'd never been in this part of Enchantia before. Why had the magic brought her here?

"Rosa!"

Rosa looked around to see Nutmeg, the fairy of the spices, standing at the top of the cliff, being blown about by the gusts of wind.

"Hi, Nutmeg!" Rosa called.

Nutmeg came scrambling down the cliff. She reached the bottom and ran over. She hugged Rosa. "I'm very glad you've come, Rosa."

"It's freezing here!" said Rosa, hugging her back.

Nutmeg nodded. "There's stormy weather all the time at the moment – because King Tristan has fallen out with King Neptune... A few days ago, Neptune's special sceptre was stolen; he was so angry that he sent storms all over the land. Everyone is really miserable because it's too windy to dance outside, and the thunder drowns out any music inside so we can't dance anywhere!"

"Well, why doesn't King Tristan just give it back?" asked Rosa.

"Because he hasn't got it," said Nutmeg. "He didn't take it. He's got absolutely no idea where it is. The only way to stop the storms is to find the sceptre and give it back. Everyone's been looking and no one has found it yet. I just don't know what we're going to do..."

°⸰⁕ ☆ ⸰⁕ ☆ ⸰⁕ ☆ ⸰⁕ °

Magic Ballerina

Darcey Bussell

Buy more great Magic Ballerina books direct from HarperCollins
at 10% off recommended retail price.
FREE postage and packing in the UK.

Delphie and the Magic Ballet Shoes	ISBN 978 0 00 728607 2
Delphie and the Magic Spell	ISBN 978 0 00 728608 9
Delphie and the Masked Ball	ISBN 978 0 00 728610 2
Delphie and the Glass Slipper	ISBN 978 0 00 728617 1
Delphie and the Fairy Godmother	ISBN 978 0 00 728611 9
Delphie and the Birthday Show	ISBN 978 0 00 728612 6
Rosa and the Secret Princess	ISBN 978 0 00 730029 7
Rosa and the Golden Bird	ISBN 978 0 00 730030 3
Rosa and the Magic Moonstone	ISBN 978 0 00 730031 0
Rosa and the Special Prize	ISBN 978 0 00 730032 7
Rosa and the Magic Dream	ISBN 978 0 00 730033 4
Rosa and the Three Wishes	ISBN 978 0 00 730034 1

All priced at £3.99

To purchase by Visa/Mastercard/Switch simply call
08707871724 or fax on **08707871725**

To pay by cheque, send a copy of this form with a cheque made payable to
'HarperCollins Publishers' to: Mail Order Dept. (Ref: BOB4),
HarperCollins Publishers, Westerhill Road, Bishopbriggs, G64 2QT,
making sure to include your full name, postal address and phone number.

From time to time HarperCollins may wish to use your personal data
to send you details of other HarperCollins publications and offers.
If you wish to receive information on other HarperCollins publications
and offers please tick this box ☐

Do not send cash or currency. Prices correct at time of press.
Prices and availability are subject to change without notice.
Delivery overseas and to Ireland incurs a £2 per book postage and packing charge.